D0351384

Tiptoe
the Magic Ballet Pony

522 772 24 4

For Elsi Rose, with her twinkle toes – SK
To Flo love from Tatine x – ST

SIMON AND SCHUSTER
First published in Great Britain in 2015 by Simon and Schuster UK Ltd
1st Floor, 222 Gray's Inn Road, London WC1X 8HB
A CBS Company
Text copyright © 2015 Sarah KilBride
Illustrations copyright © 2015 Sophie Tilley
Concept © 2009 Simon and Schuster UK
The right of Sarah KilBride and Sophie Tilley to be identified
as the author and illustrator of this work has been asserted by them
in accordance with the Copyright, Designs and Patents Act, 1988
All rights reserved, including the right of reproduction in whole or in part in any form
A CIP catalogue record for this book is available from the British Library upon request
PB ISBN: 978-0-85707-964-0
eBook ISBN: 978-0-85707-965-7
Printed in China
1 3 5 7 9 10 8 6 4 2

Princess Evie's Ponies

Tiptoe the Magic Ballet Pony

Sarah KilBride

Illustrated by Sophie Tilley

SIMON AND SCHUSTER

London New York Sydney Toronto New Delhi

The mornings were getting colder at Starlight Stables, so Princess Evie was making sure her ponies were warm and snug in their winter rugs.

"Shall we ride through the tunnel of trees today, Tiptoe?" Evie whispered.

You see, Princess Evie's ponies weren't any old ponies. Whenever she rode them through the tunnel of trees she was whisked away on a magical adventure to a faraway land.

Evie led her pretty palomino into the yard and saddled her up.
Tiptoe whinnied excitedly. She loved going on adventures,
and so did Evie's kitten, Sparkles.

"I mustn't forget this, Sparkles!" said Evie,
putting on her rucksack of useful things.
"We never know when we might need it."

Soon Tiptoe was making her
way towards the tunnel of trees.
Where would it take them today?

Tiptoe trotted out on to a beautiful stage, her bridle shimmered with
crystal stars and her hooves glittered. There was a little ballerina waiting
for them in a tutu just like Evie's made with sparkling petals.

Each of them had ballet shoes tied with new ribbons and a tiara.

"I'm Grace," she said. "Would you like to dance in tonight's show?"

"I've never been in a ballet," replied Evie.

"It'll be fun!" smiled Grace. "Follow me."

The little ballerina led them to the rehearsal room where the Sugar Plum Fairy was practising her solo. Her face lit up when she saw Evie and Tiptoe. "How wonderful you've come!" she said.

"Could your pony pull the sleigh for tonight's finale as our ballet pony has a chill?"

Tiptoe stamped her hoof excitedly. "She'd love to!" smiled Evie.

"When Tiptoe pulls us onto the stage, snowflakes will begin to fall,"
said Grace. "Then we'll perform our dance."

Evie learnt the steps quickly. First a tendu, then a passé, an arabesque, a plié, a dégagé and finally a relevé.

"I hope I can remember them all," said Evie.

"I don't want to let you down."

"You won't – you'll be a star!"

said Grace.

The girls quickly put on their stage make-up, but when Evie looked at her reflection in the dressing room mirror, her tummy fluttered uneasily. What if she fell over? What if she forgot the steps?

"Only ten minutes to go!" smiled Grace.

Before Evie had time to feel any more nervous, the door flew open and the Sugar Plum Fairy burst in.

"We've run out of snowflakes," she said. "The show will be ruined!"

"I might have something," said Evie opening her rucksack.

Sparkles dived in and pulled out sheets of white paper.

"Well done, Sparkles," laughed Evie. "Just the thing!"

They set to work and soon they'd cut a pile of tiny paper snowflakes. "Thank you, girls," said the Sugar Plum Fairy. "You've saved the show!"

And with that she rushed off. Evie could hear the audience coming into the theatre and felt her heart beating fast.

The orchestra began to play and as Evie waited nervously in the wings,
Tiptoe gently nuzzled up to her, calming her nerves.

"Thank you, Tiptoe, you're right," said Evie.

"I'm sure I'll be fine once I'm on stage."

The audience gasped as Tiptoe drew the Sugar Plum Fairy's glittering sleigh onto the stage in a flurry of snowflakes.

The Sugar Plum Fairy and Grace smiled but poor Evie froze with terror. She was dazzled by the lights and couldn't move!

It was time to dance but the Sugar Plum Fairy could see that Evie had stage fright. She pirouetted over and waved her wand.

A single star floated from its tip and landed softly on Evie's head.

Instantly, Evie felt brave and all the dance steps came flooding back to her.

The moment the orchestra played the first few notes,
Evie smiled and began to dance. The audience was spellbound.

The ballet was a fantastic success and when it finished the audience clapped and called 'Bravo!'

All the dancers curtsied deeply. The Sugar Plum Fairy was presented with a beautiful bouquet of flowers. Grace and Evie were given pretty winter posies, and even Tiptoe had a garland of red roses.

"Thank you both for such a perfect performance,"
said the Sugar Plum Fairy.
"We mustn't forget Tiptoe," added Grace.
"She was the star of the show!"

As everyone waved goodbye from the stage door, huge snowflakes fell
from the sky, covering everything in a soft blanket of white.

"Come back soon!" called Grace,
as Tiptoe and Evie trotted away and back
towards the tunnel of trees.

Starlight Stables was covered with an icy frost.

"What a magical night," said Evie as she picked up Tiptoe's winter rug.

There, underneath the rug was a pair of satin ballet shoes.

"With some practice, perhaps I'll be able to dance like the Sugar Plum Fairy one day," said Evie. "Thank you, Grace, and thank you, Tiptoe, what a very special ballet pony!"

"Miaow," agreed Sparkles, as he snuggled up on his warm blanket.

Also available:

Neptune the Magic Sea Pony

Silver the Magic Snow Pony

Willow the Magic Forest Pony

Star the Magic Sand Pony

Shimmer the Magic Ice Pony

Indigo the Magic Rainbow Pony

Diamond the Magic Unicorn

Confetti the Magic Wedding Pony

Sprinkles the Magic Cupcake Pony

Coming soon:

Melody the Magic Music Pony